Dear Parents:

Congratulations! Your child is taking the first steps on an exciting journey. The destination? Independent reading!

STEP INTO READING® will help your child get there. The program offers five steps to reading success. Each step includes fun stories and colorful art or photographs. In addition to original fiction and books with favorite characters, there are Step into Reading Non-Fiction Readers, Phonics Readers and Boxed Sets, Sticker Readers, and Comic Readers—a complete literacy program with something to interest every child.

Learning to Read, Step by Step!

Ready to Read Preschool–Kindergarten
• big type and easy words • rhyme and rhythm • picture clues
For children who know the alphabet and are eager to begin reading.

Reading with Help Preschool–Grade 1
• basic vocabulary • short sentences • simple stories
For children who recognize familiar words and sound out new words with help.

Reading on Your Own Grades 1–3
• engaging characters • easy-to-follow plots • popular topics
For children who are ready to read on their own.

Reading Paragraphs Grades 2–3
• challenging vocabulary • short paragraphs • exciting stories
For newly independent readers who read simple sentences with confidence.

Ready for Chapters Grades 2–4
• chapters • longer paragraphs • full-color art
For children who want to take the plunge into chapter books but still like colorful pictures.

STEP INTO READING® is designed to give every child a successful reading experience. The grade levels are only guides; children will progress through the steps at their own speed, developing confidence in their reading.

Remember, a lifetime love of reading starts with a single step!

Visit us on the Web!
StepIntoReading.com
randomhousekids.com

Educators and librarians, for a variety of teaching tools, visit us at RHTeachersLibrarians.com

ISBN 978-1-101-93684-9 (trade) — ISBN 978-1-101-93687-0 (lib. bdg.)

Printed in the United States of America

10 9 8 7 6 5 4 3 2 1

by Mary Tillworth
illustrated by MJ Illustrations

Random House New York

The PAW Patrol pups

are in a play.

They wear costumes.

Chase is the king.
The other pups
are knights.

Captain Turbot builds
a castle for the play.
He hammers
one last nail.

The castle falls!

Captain Turbot is stuck.

He calls the

PAW Patrol for help.

Ryder and his pups
race to the rescue!

They are ready
to help Captain Turbot.

Rubble lifts
the castle wall.

Chase pulls
the castle tower
off the captain.

Marshall x-rays
Captain Turbot.
Whew!
No broken bones!

Now the pups
must fix the castle.
Skye flies a wall
into place.

Rocky screws a door onto the wall.

Marshall and Ryder

paint the castle.

The castle is finished!

The play can start.

Chase begins to cough.

Marshall checks him out.

Chase is sick!

Ryder asks Marshall

to play the king.

The play begins.
A princess is trapped
in the tower.
A king must save her.

The pup who can
pull the bone
from the stone
will become king!

Marshall tries.
He pulls the bone.
It hits the tower!

The princess falls
from the tower!

Marshall catches
the princess!
What a good pup!

Lady Skye puts a crown on Marshall's head.

Hooray!
The king saved the day.
And Marshall saved
the play!